CHARLES DARWIN,
the Adventurer

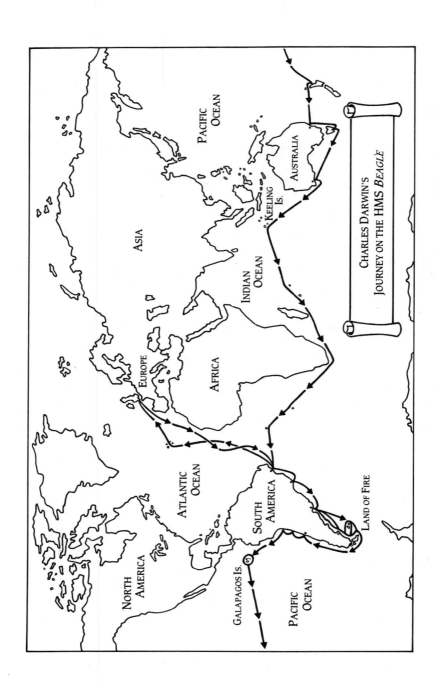

CHARLES DARWIN'S JOURNEY ON THE HMS *BEAGLE*

CHARLES DARWIN, the Adventurer

Vargie Johnson

VANTAGE PRESS
New York

Illustrated by John Flagg

Published by Vantage Press, Inc.
516 West 34th Street, New York, New York 10001

Manufactured in the United States of America
ISBN: 0-533-10092-5

Library of Congress Catalog Card No.: 91-91319

0 9 8 7 6 5 4 3 2 1

To my wife, editor,
companion, and friend:
Pamela Johnson

Contents

Acknowledgements

As background reading material the author wishes to acknowledge the following:

- *The Origin*, a biographical novel of Charles Darwin by Irving Stone (New York, Doubleday, 1980).
- *Darwin and the Enchanted Isles*, by Irwin Shapiro (Toronto, Longman Canada, Ltd., 1977).

CHARLES DARWIN,
the Adventurer

Chapter One
Books in the Attic

It was a warm spring morning. The dark-haired little boy sat on the floor of his father's waiting room browsing through old medical journals. His father was the local doctor in Shrewsbury, so there were always a lot of books and journals lying about for the boy to browse through. Mostly he liked looking at the pictures. A picture of a strange-looking beetle caught the boy's attention. Seven-year-old Charles Robert Darwin intently studied the picture of the beetle.

Charles had never been interested in beetles before, but this one took his fancy.

"I wonder," Charles spoke aloud to himself, "where on earth could one find a creature such as this?"

It was such a strange-looking animal, with two curious eyes poking out. An armoured plate covered the beetle's head, giving it the appearance of a medieval knight. But what really drew Charles's attention to the picture was the ferocious-looking horn that protruded out from the beetle's head.

Charles made up his mind then and there that one day he was going to find one of these creatures and keep it as a pet. Then whenever Sarah Parker, his next-door neighbour, came over to annoy him, he could scare her away with it.

Charles was so engrossed in what he was thinking that he lost track of the time.

"I hope you are not still in there, Charles!" came a shout

from the room next-door. "You know how your father feels about you being seen around the waiting room at this time of the morning."

Mrs. Coxsley, his father's receptionist and nurse, came through the door into the waiting room where Charles was.

"What are you doing in here then, chappie? You should be outside enjoying this lovely morning. It's a beautiful day with lots of fresh air about, and all young boys such as yourself should be outside in it. Now be off with you, lad."

"Wait, Mrs. Coxsley; come and have a look at this beetle."

"If you ask me, there should be a law against beetles that look like that. I hope nobody gets it into their mind to bring a thing like that here to England."

"Oh, I'd love to have one. Where do you think they live?"

"Strange child. Now out you go. Oh, my goodness, just look at the time."

It was ten o'clock. At precisely the stroke of ten, Mrs. Coxsley would open the doors to the surgery to allow the public into the waiting room. Charles's father had told him many times that he was never to be found in the waiting room when his patients came in to see him.

Dr. Robert Waring Darwin was very proud of the fact that he had earned for himself the reputation of being the very best doctor in town. Wealthy people from all over Shrewsbury and various other counties throughout England came to consult with him. His diagnosis was well-respected by his patients. Consequently, he ran his surgery to a strict timetable. He liked things to go exactly as planned, and he hated impunctuality. He became cross with people who were late for their appointment and would occasionally refuse to see them.

Charles knew that if his father were to find him here at

this time, he would be in big trouble, so he slipped out the back door before his father came in to greet the first patients of the day. He hid the medical journal with the picture of the beetle within the folds of his vest coat so that he could continued looking at it in his room.

"Why would a beetle of this nature develop such an unusual-looking horn?" Charles asked himself, as he lay on his bed studying the picture.

As had happened so many times before, Charles found himself deep in thought, allowing his mind to drift off to far-away places, imagining himself capturing and studying creatures similar to the one that he had in the picture before him now.

Charles lived with his mother and father in a very old but distinguished-looking house in an exclusive area of Shrewsbury, a large brick house, with several high gables and chimneys on its roof. In front of the house grew two very large oak trees. The house has a very long history going back several centuries.

Dr. Darwin bought the house not because of its history, but because it was located on the corner of two main streets. Each street contained a major entrance into the house. One door was used by patients entering the surgery, and the other was used by Charles and his family. There was a small back entrance as well, but this was used only by the day servants.

Charles loved this old house. He didn't care that the neighbours called it old and ugly and not befitting their particular area of town. He spent many hours exploring its many rooms and corridors. Upstairs, in one of the deserted rooms, the previous owner had left behind hundreds of old books, left for the mice and the dust to take care of. It was here that Charles spent all of his spare time.

"Father," Charles asked one day, "do you think I could

use some of the pictures that are in those old books up in the attic?"

His father gave him permission to use the books in whatever way he saw fit. This really excited Charles, because he loved to collect pictures and then paste them into his scrapbook. He liked to cut out pictures of animals, and he had quite an extensive collection of them. He had one on birds and another on butterflies. Any pictures of insects he came across also went into a scrapbook. His picture collection of fish included both freshwater fish and fish from the sea.

Charles then became interested in plants, so he started a brand-new scrapbook on leaves and flowers. He particularly liked the unusual-looking varieties. Then he started another scrapbook on trees. He liked to compare their likenesses and their differences. The books in the attic held a wealth of information for him. Then during the long summer days he would go out into the parks and collect leaves from different trees, bring them home, and try to identify them.

The young Darwin boy wanted to know about everything around him related to plants and animals. He looked and listened and asked countless questions. He wandered freely around the town and would frequently visit the local farms. He would sit on the edge of the canal and examine every last item that grew around him or that happened to pass by him. To young Charles Darwin, born on February 12, 1809, in Shrewsbury, England, his hometown was a wonderful place.

His mother, whose name was Susannah Wedgwood before she married his father, was a very happy woman. She had everything a woman could want: a fine husband who was respected by the whole community, a lovely big house with a lot of servants, and a beautiful, healthy child by the name of Charles.

Mrs. Darwin was the daughter of Josiah Wedgwood, a

famous potter in England. He had invented the clays and glazes needed for the preparation of making high-grade pottery. People began calling this type of pottery Wedgwood, and it ranked among the finest pottery in the world. People from all over Europe came to buy Mr. Josiah Wedgwood's pottery.

In spite of all the wonderful things Mrs. Darwin had, she was a shy and timid person. She was proud of her husband Robert's achievements and was sure that Charles, like his father, would do important things one day.

Charles's collection of pictures grew and grew, and before long he had so many they began to fill up his bedroom. He had no more room on his shelves to stack them.

It was about this time that his father started complaining that Charles was spending far too much time with his collections. One night after dinner Mr. Darwin said, "Charles, I haven't seen you reading any of my medical journals lately."

Charles knew what was coming and tried to avoid the subject. "No, Father, I haven't. I'm not really interested in reading them anymore."

Mr. Darwin, on hearing Charles's response, became quite cross and insisted that from now on Charles's time would be put to better use.

It was then that Mr. Darwin decided that the books in the upstairs room were now "off-limits" to Charles. Instead, he was only allowed to read his father's medical books. Mr. Darwin thought that Charles was now old enough to prepare himself for his chosen future career. He decided that Charles would follow in his own footsteps and become a physician one day.

So Charles was forced to read medical books and journals before he was old enough to start school. He found the books terribly boring, and the thought of becoming a doctor, like his father, didn't interest him at all. Not wanting to displease his father, Charles pretended to read them.

Visitors often came to their household at night to speak to Mr. Darwin. They were usually doctors from the local hospital, who had come to talk over a particular medical case with him. Charles looked forward to such visitors because it meant a welcome break from the boring books he had to read. Occasionally his father would insist that he be present during their conversations so that he might learn a thing or two from what they had to say. But usually he was sent to his room to be out of the way.

This he loved most of all, because it meant being with his collections of pictures. He learned their names by heart, and he learned about the countries they came from. He knew what type of environment each particular animal or plant preferred.

Most of his pictures were in black and white, so he decided one day to add colour to them, using his coloured charcoal and pencils.

He loved to add colour to his butterfly pictures most of all. He felt that they looked so much prettier that way. Occasionally he would spot one flying around in his mother's garden. He would rush outside, capture it, then return to his room to draw it and record its colour. He would take extreme care to make sure he copied it correctly.

Charles missed the books in the attic very much. No amount of talking could persuade his father to change his mind about allowing him free access to them. So Charles had to rely on his memory for the names of any new butterflies he happened to find.

Erasmus Darwin was Charles's grandfather. Although Charles had never met his grandfather, he had heard about him from his parents. Erasmus Darwin died in 1802, seven years before Charles was born. Like Charles's father, he was also a prominent physician. But more important to Charles was that his grandfather was also a naturalist. He had a great fondness for plants and animals. Charles wondered if his grandfather had had a picture collection as large as his own. His father told him that he did not.

Erasmus Darwin had collected real, live specimens. He captured them, treated them, then had them mounted for his own collection. He travelled everywhere in search of butterflies, beetles, grasshoppers, snails, birds, plants, and anything else that he could get his hands on.

There were people who accused Erasmus of spending more time in pursuit of wild creatures than in his own doctor's surgery. But to Erasmus it did not matter. He claimed he felt better at home with animals and plants than he did with his own patients. Charles loved to hear people say this. He, himself, loved his own picture collection more than anything else in the world.

Among the many talents his grandfather possessed was an art for writing poetry. He wrote very lengthy poems about nature and had them published in a couple of books. Charles had a copy of both his books and would try to read them. Although he was still too young to understand what his grandfather had written, he still liked to finger through the pages and try to recognise some of the words.

Chapter Two
School for Thought

On the morning of his first day of school, Charles was so excited that he couldn't eat his breakfast. He was dressed in a lovely new costume of grey. Both his shirt and pants were so well starched that they felt as firm as cardboard. His black leather shoes with large silver buckles in front were so shiny that he could see his own reflection in them, and his stockings were drawn right up to his knees. On this particular morning he felt really grown up. At last, he was eight years old, old enough to go to school.

Before Charles left for school, he presented himself to his father for final inspection.

"Do you think I look acceptable, Father? I'm supposed to wear this school cap, but I think it looks a little funny."

On the right hand pocket of his blazer jacket Charles proudly displayed the monogram of Doctor Butler's Private School.

"You look very handsome, young man," said Mr. Darwin, with a smile that reached from one ear to the other, pretending to brush dust off the monogram. He straightened the boy's cap and wished him all the best.

"You go and learn all you can, young man, and one day you will become a doctor just as famous as your father and grandfather."

Charles, not wanting to upset him, replied, "Yes, Father."

It was a little after eight o'clock in the morning when Charles left home for school. The gentle sun had been up for several hours, and the dew had dried off the grass, except in the shaded areas beside buildings and under trees. Charles knew these cobblestone streets very well. He had walked them many times before when searching for butterflies and beetles. Often when out wandering he would find himself passing by the local school and would occasionally stop and watch the children at play.

The school was next to the grocery store, which had two wooden benches outside for passersby to rest upon. Charles already knew that these benches were "out-of-bounds" to the children of the school.

Next to the school on the other side stood the Church of England and the vicarage, with its open-style verandah in front. It was here that the Shrewsbury Women's Benevolent Society would meet every Sunday after service, for tea and sandwiches.

On the opposite side of the road stood Mr. Linburn's blacksmith shop and barn, with his stable behind it. Often schoolchildren could be found there before and after school hand-feeding the horses that had been brought in to be shod.

In front of the school, within the school grounds, stood the flagpole. From its top a very new-looking Union Jack fluttered in the gentle breeze of the morning. Behind the flagpole on a curved wooden structure hung the big school bell.

Charles was so excited to be in school he could hardly contain himself. He thought that finally he could get to know all there is to know about plants and animals. He was sure he would learn something new about them every day.

"Good morning, Charles Robert Darwin. My name is

Mr. Robertson. I understand that this is your first day at school. Most welcome, child. Do your work carefully and correctly, and we will have no need for complaint."

"Yes, sir. Yes, Mr. Robertson."

Charles was taken to the youngest children's classroom and placed into a double desk in the back row. He took in everything that was around him, including the displays that were pinned on the wall.

Charles passed the morning in a haze of bewilderment, not understanding anything that was said or done. He was disappointed that none of the wall displays or books that he was given to look at had anything in them on plants or animals.

It wasn't until just before lunch that he noticed whom he was sharing the desk with. As a token of friendship, he invited the boy to his house.

"Hello, my name is Charles. Would you like to come and look for beetles with me after we've eaten lunch?"

"No! I think beetles are nasty and shouldn't be allowed upon this earth. They should all be found and stepped on."

Charles was shocked beyond belief at the boy's reply, so he asked Mr. Robertson, his teacher, what he thought about beetles. Mr. Robertson was furious with Charles for speaking of such things during arithmetic time and had nothing to say on the matter.

It became obvious to Charles that none of the children in the class were interested in joining him at lunchtime to look for bugs, butterflies, or even plants. They laughed at him when he told them about his collection of pictures and told him that they had better things to do with their spare time.

When the bell rang for afternoon classes, Charles joined the end of the line as they filed into school one by one. He felt very sad and disappointed. He had come to school eager

11

to make friends and to share his interests with other boys. Instead nobody wanted to know him.

Charles began to realise that he was different from everyone else. Nobody was interested in the things he was interested in. His father was displeased with him for spending so much time with his collections. His teacher had nothing to say on the matter, and the children in his class thought that he was a little strange for having such interests.

Charles made up his mind on that first day of school that he was going to learn about plants and animals in his own way. Silently. He wouldn't share his collection with anyone.

As the days grew into months he learned to ignore his fellow students' remarks.

"What did you have for breakfast this morning, Darwin? Beetle juice!"

"Brought any of your crawling friends to school today, Darwin?"

However, the unintelligible things that Mr. Robertson was always writing on the blackboard gradually began to make sense. Charles learned that a "+" meant that you counted all the numbers up and totalled them. Where there was a "-" sign, that meant that you took the numbers on the bottom away from the numbers on the top.

Charles was a bright boy and would have been an excellent student, had he overcome the constant snickering and pestering the rest of the children gave him. He was labelled on that first day of school "the nature nut." Consequently, any jokes or sarcastic comments concerning anything to do with animals or plants were directed at him. Whenever this would happen he would completely forget about his schoolwork and withdraw into himself. Inevitably, he would start doing untidy writing or would start sketching an animal of some kind on his slate. As a result it was always his slate that Mr. Robertson held up to sneer at and be used to demonstrate the ugliness of untidy work. It seemed to Charles that he was always quivering under Mr. Robertson's sarcastic remarks or blushing bright red because the rest of the class was laughing at him.

As the years passed, Charles's reports and grades went from bad to worse. His father became extremely angry with him.

"I don't know what to do with you, Charles. You don't seem to understand that in order to make it in this world, you have to work very hard. You are becoming an embarrassment to me. Please try harder!"

It became a common occurrence for Mr. Darwin to cancel a block of appointments with patients so that he could attend Doctor Butler's Private School to discuss Charles's behaviour. They told Mr. Darwin that Charles was not performing up to standard and would have to be removed from school if he did not improve.

That day did come, seven years after Charles first entered the school. Charles's teacher at the time was giving a lesson on botany, the study of plants. He made a statement saying how wonderful it is that right from the beginning God created all living things so perfect and so unique from each other. Charles did not agree with this theory at all and stood up and told the teacher so.

"What a load of rubbish. Sir! As a teacher you shouldn't be making statements like that."

A classroom full of shocked students listened in silence as Charles and the teacher argued the point.

"A statement of this nature is of a private opinion and should remain so. You are not allowing the boys in this class to think for themselves," Charles said.

The teacher sent Charles home for insubordination. As a result of this, Mr. Darwin withdrew Charles from Doctor Butler's Private School. He accused Charles of being a lazy, idlesome person, a disgrace to himself and to all his family. Mr. Darwin was very disappointed with his son and confined him to his room until he could think of what he was going to do with him next.

Charles was happy to be out of that school and felt that he had learned very little there anyway. They stopped him from doing the things he wanted to do. Beside, what good is a school that does not teach nature study?

Chapter Three
A Dream of Being Famous

Not too long after his sixteenth birthday, in 1825, Charles was taken away from home and sent to Edinburgh. His father wanted him to become a doctor, so he was sent to Scotland to study medicine. Charles had never been to such a big city before. He saw theatres there, fine shops, and crowds of people dressed in fancy clothes, ladies in their stylish gowns and sleek furs and the men in glossy hats and fine suits. *What a busy place,* thought Charles, and he wondered whether or not he was going to like it here.

"Hey, you! Watch out, fool!" yelled the driver of a passing horse-drawn cart.

"You had better watch where you're going, young man. You were nearly run over by those horses."

Charles was so caught up with the commotion of the city that he completely forgot to watch out for the horse traffic on the busy Edinburgh streets.

"Yes, I suppose you're right, madam," replied Charles, as he continued to cross the street.

He couldn't get over the amount of people there were here, all busily going about their business. He wondered what they were all doing and why they all seem to be in so much of a hurry, a far cry from his hometown of Shrewsbury.

Charles soon found his prearranged lodgings and enrolled at the University of Edinburgh, as his father wished, and began studying medicine. But he found the long lectures tiresome and the subject matter boring. He couldn't make up his mind which was worse, Doctor Butler's Private School or here at Edinburgh. After school, long hours of study were required of him, but he found that he just could not concentrate. As a substitute for studying he began to take long walks in the parks and read books about nature.

While out walking he began collecting caterpillars and keeping them in glass jars in his room. From reading books on insects he knew exactly what these caterpillars ate, so fed each one a diet of its favorite leaves.

He had patiently watched each caterpillar as it changed into its next stage, the chrysalis. Then finally when each chrysalis would split open, he would become completely absorbed in what was happening, sitting through the long, slow process that followed. It never ceased to amaze him how this wet, curled-up, shapeless insect slowly pulled itself out of the chrysalis, stretched and smoothed out its wrinkled wings, and became transformed into a beautiful full-blown butterfly.

Charles became more and more involved with his little friends so that he completely ignored his studies. He disliked medicine and began skipping classes and would fail to turn up for important demonstrations. He could not bear to even watch operations, which were still performed without anaesthesia.

He turned more and more to his little friends for comfort. As well as caterpillars he would bring home frogs and big toads, birds, small snakes, and crickets and other insects. He would even bring cats and homeless dogs back to be fed. Friends and neighbours who dropped in to visit Charles often shrieked in fright when they saw the amount of wildlife he had scattered around the room.

"Charles, you have to be crazy to keep all these animals here in this room. If you spent as much time studying as you do with these creatures, you'd be a brilliant doctor someday."

Charles had heard remarks like this before from his father. So to avoid similar comments from fellow students, he would slip away during week-ends when most of them were studying or catching up on schoolwork. Charles would take excursions out of town to visit the rolling hill country. He loved the rural area and found great excitement in watching the seasons change.

While out in the woods he began to mimic birds and would occasionally catch them by imitating their song. He'd give them to the local children as pets after teaching the little ones how to handle them. He also taught them about plants, how to recognise potentially dangerous ones. And he even found time to help plant and weed the neighbours' vegetable garden.

By the time Charles was seventeen years old he dreamed that one day he would become a great authority on animals and plants. He would travel to jungles in foreign lands to collect rare species. Maybe he'd publish a book or two on the subject and become very famous. When he told his friends about his dream, they laughed at him and said he couldn't even complete a term paper at university, let alone write a book on animals and plants.

When Charles wasn't in class or attending to his animal friends, he went walking around the city. Edinburgh fascinated him. There was always something worth looking at or listening to on the streets of the big city. There were all those busy people, coming and going, walking fast, always in a hurry. Horse-drawn carriages moved in all directions, transporting people from one place to the other.

He loved to look in the store windows, although they were not the kind of stores to which he was accustomed. He would walk carefully down the street going from one window to the next. He enjoyed the tobacconist's store, with its aroma of exotic tobacco, and the eating houses, some of them with their menus displayed on the door. He was shocked at the prices. He marvelled at the stores that only sold one or two products. Some sold nothing but umbrellas, Persian carpets, or conjuring tricks. Charles spent a long time at that window, studying the false noses, moustaches, beards, and joke kits.

He came upon a store that sold nothing but lollie-sticks and ice cream; the sign above the store said over eight different varieties. Charles went in and stared at the glass cases displaying the ice cream. The trouble was he could not make up his mind which to have. He eventually decided upon a plain variety that was full of nuts, so he paid his penny, collected his ice cream, and left the store.

"Is that you, young Charles? You out walking the streets again?" shouted one of the storekeepers, with whom Charles had now become acquainted.

"How can you expect to become a great doctor walking the streets eating ice cream?"

Charles waved and gave him a friendly grin and walked on down the street munching away and deep in thought. He thought about his fellow students in class, working hard in preparation for their second-year medical examinations. He thought about the city he was in and whether or not he wanted to study here any longer. He thought about his father, who would be extremely angry with him, if he knew that he was out on the streets wasting time. And he thought about the career that his father has chosen for him and decided that a career of medicine was not what he wanted.

The problem now was how to tell his father this. Charles knew that his father had placed great hopes in him keeping up the family tradition and becoming a doctor. He made up his mind right then and there to return to his room and write his father a letter.

Chapter Four
Scientists and Sportsmen

Mr. Darwin read the letter. He was far too angry to speak. Eventually, his anger gradually turned to disappointment. He realised that his son was a failure, and he wondered what was to become of him. He had hoped that the last two years in Edinburgh would have taught Charles something, but he realised that it had all been a waste of time.

Mr. Darwin's final solution for Charles was the church. He would send him to a school that would train him to become a clergyman. In 1827, Charles was withdrawn from Edinburgh University and sent to Christ's College in Cambridge, to prepare him for Holy Orders into the Church of England.

Charles knew that rich families often used the church as a last resort for their children they felt were failing. He didn't mind, though. Being in Cambridge meant that he was around new people, he was studying in an area that was new to him, and the climate was more appealing. But more important, it meant he was out of the field of medicine. He no longer had to sit through boring lectures or watch bloody operations performed without anaesthesia.

He felt studying in Cambridge offered so much more to the student. Charles became very interested in sport.

"Charles, I understand you're new in town. Have you

enlisted in any of the sports clubs posted on the board yet?" asked a fellow student during the first week of classes.

"No, as yet I haven't."

"Good. How would you like to join the swimming team with me this afternoon?"

Without giving it much thought, Charles decided to give it a try, even though he hadn't done much swimming in the past. He found he actually enjoyed the sport and began looking for other sport activities to sign up for.

It wasn't long before he became quite the sportsman on campus. In fact, he soon got the reputation of being a person that would give any sport a try. He tried everything from tennis and wrestling to swimming and rowing on the Cam River.

He hadn't been in Cambridge too long before he was invited to join the school's cricket team, being approached by the team coach, who said, "Charles, I've noticed that you've joined up with just about every sport activity possible here in Cambridge; how about giving cricket a try?"

Not knowing very much about the sport, Charles was hesitant to join. Before giving the team coach his answer he decided to do a bit of research into the game. Charles discovered that cricket originated in England as a simple bat and ball game five hundred years ago and it wasn't until the midsixteenth century that it became known as cricket. The game was now being played in all British colonies, and there were thoughts of holding international tournaments between these various colonies.

Charles decided that cricket might be just the sport for him and, to his own surprise, discovered that he was a natural at the game. He loved it. It wasn't long before he found himself selected on the team to represent their university, playing neighbouring teams.

Sport opened up a whole new world for Charles, and for

the first time in his life he was interested in something other than botany. Charles was never one for socialising or going out of his way to meet new people, but being part of the cricket team made it easy for him. He would be invited to social functions every week-end after the game was over. He enjoyed this new life of his and began to look forward to week-ends more than ever.

A relatively new sport of Cambridge was wrestling. The club was small and desperately in need of new members, so Charles decided to join. He wasn't too sure how he would make out at contact sports, but he decided to give the sport a try. Like cricket, he enjoyed it a lot and would faithfully attend the weekly meetings. It was just as well that he did, because it was at one of these meetings that he met a professor called Adam Sedgwick.

While sitting on the sidelines awaiting his turn, Charles had the good fortune to overhear a conversation between a student and another gentleman.

"I have among my collection of rocks a fossil that you might be interested in seeing," stated the gentleman.

The student, obviously pleased beyond words, replied, "That would be great. I'm sure that it would help me with my term paper. When can I see it?"

"How about coming around to my house this afternoon?"

"Forgive my rudeness and for interrupting, but I too am extremely interested in fossils. My name is Charles Darwin."

"Pleased to make your acquaintance, Charles. I'm Professor Sedgwick and this here is Ashton," replied the gentleman. "No, you're not being rude. The more people interested in rocks and fossils the better, in my view."

Charles soon discovered that Professor Sedgwick studied the rocks of the earth and was especially interested in volcanoes and earthquakes. He would invite Charles to join him on many of his long walks to collect rocks and fossils. While out walking they would discuss their surroundings, including the plants and animals. This rekindled Charles's interest in botany, which had lately been overlooked due to the number of sports Charles was involved in.

Occasionally the schools in Cambridge held track-and-field athletic events among themselves, similar to what the ancient Greeks used to do. Charles would sign up for all events whether he knew the rules or not. In addition to the simple running races, he participated in the long jump and the throwing events of javelin and discus.

Several times throughout the year, the school would hold picnics next to the river Cam, and the usual sporting activities that were connected with the picnic took place. Swimming, by far, was the most popular event of the day, with each department selecting their best swimmers to enter into a race.

Although Charles wasn't the best swimmer in his class, he still entered for the fun of it.

Punting on the Cam River was a fun activity in which everybody participated. The number of people that could fit into the boat ranged from two to as many as the boat could hold before sinking. Inevitably, boats did overturn, to the delights of the onlookers, as they cheered and yelled verbal abuse to each participant as he swam ashore.

It was during one of these picnics that Charles met a man who was to have a major effect on his life.

"Charles!" yelled Professor Sedgwick, from the banks of the Cam River. "When you're through frolicking in that water, come out and dry yourself off. I have someone here I want you to meet."

Charles had no idea he was about to meet the man that would change his life forever.

"John Stevens Henslow, meet a rather soaked Charles

Robert Darwin. Charles, I present to you a professor of botany."

Charles was beyond himself with excitement. He had so many questions he wanted to ask this expert that they all seemed to come out at once. Professor Henslow immediately took a liking to Charles, and they became instant friends and spent many hours together, both in and out of school, discussing their common interest.

Mr. Henslow very quickly saw that Charles had an incredible knowledge on the subject and thought that such a talent would be wasted in the ministry.

Actually, Charles gave little attention to his ministerial studies and spent more time with his scientist friends and young sportsmen associates. Although Charles did attend his lectures and passed most of his examinations, his heart wasn't in his work. He knew that one day he would have to disappoint his father yet again.

By 1831, when he received his B.A. from the university, Charles made up his mind that he was not going to become a clergyman. His father was a very disappointed man because he thought that Charles had let him down. Charles knew what his father's reaction would be; it had been this way since he was nine years old.

One day, John Stevens Henslow mentioned to Charles that he had heard that the HMS *Beagle* was about to leave on a scientific expedition around the world and that they were looking for a naturalist to join the ship's crew. Mr. Henslow also went on to say that he knew the ship's captain and, if Charles agreed, would recommend him for the unpaid position.

Chapter Five
HMS *Beagle*

Charles managed to obtain the position as naturalist on board the *Beagle*, and so began for him an incredible scientific voyage that was to span a period of over five eventful years. This cruise was the turning point in Charles's life, for it brought him into direct contact with nature. It gave him the opportunity to study and observe at firsthand a wide range of natural phenomena.

HMS *Beagle* was a warship, a Royal Navy sailing brig, under the command of Captain FitzRoy. Its crew members were extremely fit and agile. They needed to be, thought Charles, in order to climb to the top of the yardarms at the shrilling sound of the coxwain's pipe. Charles watched as the sailors scrambled up the high masts to check the sails that were neatly tied to the yardarms. He knew that in rough seas this could be extremely dangerous work.

As Charles stood on the docks watching the sailors go about their work, Captain FitzRoy was supervising the loading of the ship's supplies. It was hard and tedious work, as each sailor made trip after trip into the hold, carrying heavy barrels and crates full of stores that were needed for their journey. Some of the crates were labelled with signs that read: *Salted Meat, Flour, Tea, Biscuits*. Then came the wooden barrels full of fresh water that a pair of sailors could only just manage between them. Charles felt sorry for the men as he heard the captain shout, "Move along there! You're as slow as old women! And pack those barrels into the hold tight; I don't want to see an inch of wasted space."

Charles wondered if he should help but decided that he would only get in the sailors' way and would end up being shouted at by Captain FitzRoy.

December 27, 1831, the captain gave the orders: "All hands on deck, pull up the anchor, and drop those sails. South America, here we come."

As Charles explored his new surroundings, which were to be his home for the next five years, the captain set a course south-west for Brazil. Charles could sense that there were mixed feelings among the men as they pulled away from land. Some of them were very sad to be leaving family and friends for such a long time, while others were happy to be on the high seas once again. The ocean was in their blood, and they were happiest when they were upon it.

They had only been sailing for a couple of hours when Charles began to feel funny inside. His stomach felt as light as a feather, and his head became dizzy.

"What's the matter, Charles?" joked some of the sailors. "Feeling a bit seasick? Maybe he needs his mother."

"We may as well turn the ship around right now and return him home."

The sailors laughed and joked with him as the captain ordered him below. And for the next two days Charles lay in his cabin most of the time and was dreadfully seasick.

"Don't worry, Charles," Captain FitzRoy told him. "All good sailors go through this experience when they first set out. You'll gradually grow used to it, you will see."

Charles, of course, didn't believe the captain and thought that at any moment he was going to die. How could anyone ever get used to this constant rolling of the ship? But as one day grew into the next, the captain's words rang true. Charles did feel a lot better and became accustomed to the

ship's movements. He began to feel rather foolish for ever doubting the captain's words and realised that Captain Fitz-Roy was an excellent captain and an excellent sailor. A sailing ship needed a good leader like him if it was to succeed upon the oceans. A sailing ship with a poor captain was a very dangerous place to be.

During the long hours at sea Charles had a lot of time to write a diary. He kept notes on everything. He recorded the conditions of the sea and birds or fish that happened to pass by. He would even jot down weather conditions, how long they lasted, and whenever they changed.

He noted how the sailors went about their daily chores willingly, without complaining and without being told. Bad behaviour was unacceptable on board, and often sailors were flogged at the mast for their wrongdoings. Discipline on the *Beagle* was very harsh.

One day Charles had found himself a quiet corner on deck and settled down to write an entry into his diary. It was mid-February, and they had been on the seas for roughly six weeks. He was approached by several sailors.

"Forgive us, Mr. Darwin," said one of the men. "We have to do this."

Before Charles could do anything, the men had lifted him into the air, his diary and pen were being knocked down from his hands, and he was being carried up to the main deck. He saw the whole crew waiting there, rolling in fits of laughter as they saw Charles approaching. It wasn't until he saw Captain FitzRoy dressed up like King Neptune that he realised what was going on.

As Charles looked around him he realised that he wasn't the only victim being carried onto the main deck. There was great excitement as the crew giggled and bubbled over with anticipation, obviously knowing what was going to happen next.

King Neptune produced a scroll from under his costume and read out aloud: " 'As you all may or may not be aware, today we are sailing across the Equator. We shall sail from the northern half of the world to the southern half.' "

Charles knew that sailors have weird customs whenever they cross the Equator and he, along with several others, was about to suffer some of them.

"' King Neptune, with his constables, ruled over all the oceans,' " Captain FitzRoy continued. " 'They hid in dark corners and waited for unsuspecting sailors.' "

There were chuckles of delight from the onlookers, as they waited eagerly for the ceremony to commence.

Before Charles could hear any more of King Neptune's proclamations, buckets and buckets of water were being tossed over them, during which time he heard roars of laughter coming from the sailors. Before Charles could recover from the water, a shaving cream mixed with a vile-smelling oil mixture called pitch was plastered over his face. Then several of the sailors began shaving off his beard and moustache. No sooner had King Neptune's constables completed this part of the ceremony and before Charles could utter any word of protest, he found himself being tossed up into the air over and over again.

Charles felt quite relieved once they had finished with him and King Neptune was satisfied with his treatment. He saw the order given for the next victim's treatment to commence. A great cheer was given as the attention was now upon the next poor sailor.

Charles found himself drawn into the excitement of the event as he saw what was happening to the next man. He even found himself cheering the constables on. He felt he had been let off lightly, as he watched the sailor who followed him receive far worse treatment.

Chapter Six
A Botanist's Paradise

"Land ahoy!" was heard echoing around the *Beagle* that last day in February 1832. They had finally reached South America. There was great excitement on board the ship as they put in at the port of Bahia, in Brazil. Charles was anxious to go ashore to explore this new land. He had heard of strange plants that were to be found here and the equally strange edible fruit that they produced. His first stop, once he got ashore, was the marketplace in Bahia. He was amazed at what there was and came back to the ship laden down with strange-looking vegetables and exotic fruits. A couple that he was quite taken by were a long yellowish fruit they called a banana and a round ball-like fruit with an extra hard outer shell called a coconut.

"Just wait until you see what I've brought back to show you!" Charles shouted up at some of the crew as he approached the ship.

"Don't you bring those cannonballs on board," a sailor joked as they saw him carrying the coconut.

"And Captain FitzRoy, look what I've bought for you!" Charles shouted, holding up the bananas, "Just wait until you've tasted these!"

Captain FitzRoy did enjoy the taste of the new fruit, but he had a more important thought on his mind. He could now begin doing the job he was sent out here to do. He announced to his crew, "Our mission here is to sail along the coastline of certain foreign lands and take all sorts of measurements. These in turn will be used by the navy to draw good, accurate maps."

He also informed them that they had to measure the depth of the water so that charts could be drawn up, which would eventually be printed, distributed, and used by other ships, to travel more safely in the area.

"What if we encounter strange and hostile people, as we sail around this continent charting these waters, Captain FitzRoy?"

"We'll cross that bridge if and when we get to it. But I don't see that as being a problem. These waters are not known for hostility."

Charles loved being here in Brazil and would take trips every day into the rain forest. He was very impressed at what he saw. He filled notebook after notebook with his observations. He would return to ship and have the sailors spellbound as he described to them some of the things he saw.

"The Brazilian jungles are like nothing you've ever seen before," he told them. "Once under its canopy, it's like stepping into a dark room, as the huge trees blot out the sky from view. I saw every shade of green imaginable."

"What about the birds?" someone would shout.

"You've never seen birds so beautiful," Charles said, "most displaying colours as bright as the rainbow. I saw tiny little hummingbirds the size of your thumb, darting so closely around my head, as if fully aware that I would never hurt them. Their wings were beating so rapidly it was impossible to see them." Charles went on to describe some of the small insects that he had seen; he had obviously captivated his audience with the stories he was telling.

"But what impressed me most," Charles went on to say,

"was the forest floor. It was literally moving in front of my eyes. Insects of all kinds were busily going about their business. The most common I saw were the army ants, who were travelling in great numbers. They attack, and usually kill, anything that happens to get in their way. Other ants, spiders, and cockroaches and even small animals like lizards and frogs were completely overcome by the army ants if they weren't quick enough to get out of their way."

Charles could have stayed in the Brazilian rain forest forever recording and collecting samples. But Captain Fitz-Roy had his own work to do, and once he had completed measuring the area, they sailed south. In certain areas Charles would stay ashore in villages and conduct his observations and studies from there; then when the captain had completed collecting the data he needed, they would pick Charles up and move on.

He wrote many letters home to friends at Cambridge but found it almost impossible to describe the beauty of the scenery he saw.

"The forest is simply teeming with life," he wrote. "It's a botanist's paradise. I saw frogs with little suckers on their toes to help them climb plants. I saw butterflies and moths that look almost identical to each other, beetles that swim, spiders that fly, and was told by locals of fish that can strip the flesh of a whole beast in a matter of minutes."

Once Captain FitzRoy had completed his work along the coast of Brazil he headed south to Argentina. They eventually travelled on down to the very southernmost tip of the continent, to a land called Tierra del Fuego.

"Would it be possible for me to go ashore here?" Charles asked the captain.

"Only if you take several men with you for protection," replied the captain. "This area is known for its hostile tribesmen."

Charles wasn't too worried about wild tribesmen but was concerned about the harsh environment he was looking at.

After being placed ashore, Charles set off to explore the surrounding countryside. He carried nothing but a notebook and several collecting boxes. He was not as impressed with the forests here as he had been with the ones he had seen in Brazil. Because of the amount of dampness in the air, trees were lying on the forest floor soaked with moisture.

He later told the sailors back on board, "This is not a very hospitable place to be in. By the look of those thick, gloomy clouds and the amount of rotting wood on the ground, this must be the land of gales and constant rainfall."

"I hope no gales come this way while we are here," replied one of the sailors. "Can you imagine being stuck in a place like this forever and a day?"

Charles wasn't too upset when the captain announced that they were leaving for Cape Horn, although he knew that Cape Horn was considered by sailors to be the most treacherous stretch of water in the world. Charles had great faith in the captain's ability to guide the *Beagle* through the dangerous waters. He had seen him in many similar situations before.

Charles could sense the anxiety among the men as they rounded the Cape in stormy weather and biting winds. They all knew that this sea had claimed many ships in the past, and there wasn't a sailor among them that hadn't known someone, directly or indirectly, that had been on board a ship that had gone down in these waters.

"Do you think we're gong to make it?" the cabin boy asked Charles as the water began to splash over the deck.

"Of course we are. Captain FitzRoy can handle any ship in these waters. Just pray that the storm doesn't become a lot worse."

Once they rounded the Cape there was a sigh of relief by everyone as the *Beagle* headed into the great Pacific Ocean.

Captain FitzRoy wasted little time in beginning his surveying on a number of small islands and channels.

"I believe that's Chile," Charles mentioned to some of the sailors. "In an atlas you can see that this country stretches for much of the west coast of South America." Charles found it a pleasure gazing out over calm seas after what they had just come through.

It was late in July 1834 that the *Beagle* anchored in the bay of Valparaiso; of course Charles took the opportunity to go ashore. On his return the captain asked what he had seen, and he replied excitedly, "I saw these strange-looking animals the locals called armadillos, a most curious-looking creature to observe as they scuttle around with plates of armour over their backs."

"Why didn't you bring several back with you?" asked the captain. "I'm told they make good eating. The cook could have fixed us a delicious treat tonight."

"That's what the locals told me," Charles said. "Unfortunately for the little beasts, their meat make a rather tasty stew, once stripped of their plating. They are a particular favourite of the locals."

The *Beagle* continued its map work for the navy, travelling north along the coast of South America, while Mr. Darwin continued conducting his own study, observing wildlife, rocks, and plants and collecting interesting-looking specimens.

Chapter Seven
Giant Tortoises Ashore

(Galapagos Islands)

About six hundred miles off the coast of Ecuador lies the small group of volcanic islands called the Galapagos Islands. Captain FitzRoy had been ordered to survey the islands, so in early September 1835 the *Beagle* sailed away from South America and headed north-west across the Pacific. Charles was kept very busy in his cabin classifying and cataloguing his many fossils and rocks, plants and wildlife, and shells and bones that he had collected in South America. It seemed that he had so many species that he could grow his own jungle.

"Land ahoy!" bellowed the man from the lookout, perched high in the rigging. Everyone, including Charles, gazed towards the horizon, and before long the black, forlorn sight of the tops of volcanoes soon came into view.

"Do you think those are what I think they are?" asked Charles.

As the *Beagle* sailed closer into shore Charles was able to make out the uninviting, bleak landscape of the islands.

"Looks like a ghost land, if you ask me," announced one of the deckhands.

Then as the ship anchored off the coast, they could see that black lava covered the entire surface of the rocky coastline and scattered here and there grew trees that were obviously stunted by the conditions.

"How could anything possibly survive in such a place?" Charles asked a sailor standing nearby. "This has to be the last place on earth any creature would possibly choose to live."

He was to be proven wrong, though. On further inspection of the island, he discovered that the place was teeming with life, of many different varieties. In fact, he found the wildlife far more interesting here than in any other place he had visited so far on the voyage.

Captain FitzRoy allowed the men to go ashore with Charles to see what they could find. The first obstacles they encountered while trying to reach the interior of the island were the forests of giant cactuses, each plant containing many extra-long, sharp prickles that could inflict a nasty wound if it was brushed up against.

"Who on earth would want to visit an area as bleak as this? Let's make tracks and return to the *Beagle*," said Charles.

The men found that the extremely rough lava that covered the ground made walking very difficult and exhausting. Most of them began complaining and were about to turn back when someone shouted, "Oh, my goodness, what are those?"

Heading toward them and walking very slowly were several giant tortoises. They caused great excitement among the sailors. One of them decided to hop on a tortoise's back to take a ride, to see if it was strong enough to carry him. The giant tortoise carried on walking seemingly unaffected by the extra burden placed upon it.

The sailors roared with laughter as several of the men tried to lift one off its feet, but the huge creature glided slowly away.

Charles was beside himself with excitement. He had

read somewhere that these animals did exist. Never in his wildest dreams did he think that he would encounter them on this island.

"Charles, do you think that we can take one of these back to the ship to keep as a pet?" The men roared with laughter.

"Of course you can, if you can carry it."

The men ventured farther on up the hill, where they came across a half dozen more of the tortoises, resting in the sun. At first glance, they looked like boulders lying side by side.

When disturbed, a long, leathery neck would emerge, followed by four huge feet. The animal would give a couple of frightful hissing sounds and would move off, digging its enormous claws into the earth and lava to help it move along.

"Imagine having a shell as large as this on board. We could use it as a bath."

Once the men were back at the ship and were conveying their adventures to the sailors who stayed behind, they were amazed to learn from Captain FitzRoy that these giant tortoises were hunted for their meat, being killed by the hundreds.

Charles was able to spend several weeks observing and recording data on these large animals, and he soon found himself becoming quite attached to them.

On other expeditions onto the islands, Charles noted all sorts of other strange-looking creatures. He was fascinated by the huge black lizards with long tails that seemed to be comfortable both in and out of the water. During cool periods they would lie on the rocks, basking in the sun to get warm, then in the heat of the day would lie close to the water's edge clinging to the rocks, while the waves dashed over them.

Over the next five weeks the HMS *Beagle* was busy surveying the islands of the Galapagos. Charles found plenty to study. He noticed that all the islands were very similar to each other, all being volcanic and all lying virtually on the Equator. Yet the birds, tortoises, and lizards, all of which were obviously from the same species, were slightly different on each of the islands.

For instance, he noted that the finches of the same species on the various islands evolved in a certain way to suit the conditions on their particular island. For example, a finch on a particular island would only eat small seeds, so therefore its beak remained small. However, the finches on another island only had large seeds available for them to eat, so they developed a larger, stronger beak for crushing the large seeds. Then the same finches on yet another island only had insects available for them to eat, so they developed a longer, slender beak for prying into the ground.

As well as studying finches, Charles learned from the locals that the tortoises are different on each of the islands as well. The natives could tell which island they are on simply by looking at the sort of tortoise that lives there.

All of this was very puzzling for Charles, and he pondered over these differences for a very long time. He was sure that these animals started off the same on all these islands; now, all these years later, they were different. Why? He kept asking himself. What would cause these evolutionary changes? How could a seed-eating finch suddenly learn to eat larger seeds, which others could not? While others still learned how to eat insects? How could they individually develop a particular beak in a particular size and shape to eat the food that was available to them?

This was indeed very puzzling for Charles, and he returned to England in 1836 without an answer, although he thought about it all the way home.

Chapter Eight
The Long Way Home

Charles stood on the deck and bade farewell to the bleak, black islands of the Galapagos, with their strange animals. He knew that he would never have another chance to return. He also felt that over the past five weeks he had made a very great discovery and here on the Galapagos Islands he had evidence. He wasn't quite sure what it was, but he had a vague idea what it could mean.

As the *Beagle* sailed off across the Pacific Ocean, Charles couldn't help but feel a little saddened knowing that he probably would never return to these islands he had grown to love.

"Do you think we'll ever come across islands similar to these again, Charles?" asked a deckhand, as they both stood at the railing watching the volcanoes diminish from sight.

"I doubt it. But then again, I suppose we could," Charles replied, trying hard to project a little hopefulness in his voice.

As Charles returned to his cabin he had this feeling that these islands were to play a very important role in his life in the future. He couldn't pinpoint it right at the moment, but he felt that it would come.

Charles felt that his journey home was not as eventful as the voyage it took to reach the Galapagos Islands. In fact, he spent most of his time over the next few months in bed in his cabin. He had become ill from some disease that he couldn't identify. Ever since he had left the coastline of Chile, he had felt himself gradually losing strength. He knew that he was getting thinner by the way his clothes no longer fit him. They hung loosely on his body. His face also looked a little older. But he pushed himself on, knowing that every minute he had on this voyage was too precious to waste.

Charles didn't realise just how sick he was until one day, not too long after leaving the Galapagos Islands, he found himself too weak to get out of bed. Food had to be brought by the cook to Charles in his cabin. So he was forced to rest, spending day after day lying in his bed. He felt frustrated at not being able to be up and about observing his surroundings and recording fresh data.

The *Beagle*, however, sailed on, visiting exotic islands, where there was plenty to see. Just before Christmas 1835, they sighted New Zealand and landed.

"Haere mai, haere mai," came the call from off the beach as Captain FitzRoy, Charles, and several of the men rowed ashore. A group of Maori people had gathered on the beach to welcome them. They were friendly people but extremely ferocious-looking. The men had intricate designs tattooed all over their faces. The women also bore tattoos, but they were confined to the lips and chin.

It was easy to see that these people loved their food and were very good at preparing it. Charles watched as the men heated large stones over a raging fire until they were white hot. They were then placed into a hole in the earth, and baskets of food were positioned upon them. Finally, wet leaves were placed upon the food. Earth was piled high on top of the whole preparation, trapping the moisture inside to cook the food slowly. Three to four hours later out came the food, so succulent that it was very hard to refuse. The Maori called this the *hangi* feast. The crew off the *Beagle* was treated

to many such feasts over the few days that they were in this land.

Although their visit to New Zealand was short, Charles was able to learn a few Maori words and phrases from their hosts.

"Tena koe, Charles. Kei te pehea koe?"

Charles learned that this was a greeting.

"Hello, how are you?" everyone said to him. Someone had taught him that the reply was: "Kei te pai." Very well, thank you.

Nowhere had the hospitality been as great as it had been here in New Zealand.

"Haere ra. Charles."

"Hei konei ra."

"Hoki mai, apopo."

"Good-bye, Charles"; "Farewell"; "Come back tomorrow"; these were the parting words from these people as the ship left the shores of New Zealand.

Charles could have stayed with the Maori for months, except the captain was anxious to move on.

Australia was sighted a few days later, in the new year of 1836. But as in New Zealand, Captain FitzRoy only stayed anchored in Sydney Harbour for a few days before beginning his crossing of the Indian Ocean.

Charles spent many hours pondering over his notes. He kept thinking about the observations he had made on the Galapagos Islands and about the theory that living things change over the course of time to suit their environment. It wasn't a new idea, he had heard of others who thought this way, but they had been ridiculed by the public for having such outrageous ideas. But on the Galapagos there was the living proof that this was so, animals and plants did change to suit their environment. Charles would sit up at night after everyone had gone to bed, thinking about this theory.

Around the beginning of April 1836, the *Beagle* sighted Keeling Island, which, Charles later found, was composed entirely of coral.

"Isn't it amazing, Captain, that a community such as this can live on an island built up entirely of coral? My friends back in England won't believe me when I tell them about this," he said to the captain.

"Aye, boy, you might be right there. So you make sure that you record every last detail about this place in those books of yours."

Like the Maori in New Zealand, the islanders here were extremely hospitable, generous people and welcomed the crew with warm, friendly smiles. They stayed on the islands for several days enjoying the comforts the islanders had to offer. The lagoons that surrounded the island made fishing exciting. The water was so clear one could virtually see the fish swimming towards the hook. Turtles occasionally swam into the lagoon and, if captured by the locals, soon were turned into turtle soup. The islanders had a hundred and one uses for the coconuts that grew in abundance on their island.

Everyone knew that their stay here on the Keeling Islands was to be a short one as well, as the captain was eager to reach England as quickly as possible.

So the *Beagle* continued her voyage across the Indian Ocean, sailing very near to Madagascar, around the southern tip of Africa, then across the southern Atlantic Ocean. They were heading back to Brazil and, in particular, Bahia, where four and a half years earlier they had first lain at anchor.

"Who would have thought this possible? Back in Brazil after sailing right the way around the world," remarked a sailor standing on deck.

In August they left Brazil knowing that they were definitely now on the last leg of their journey. It would only take two months to reach England, although everyone knew that it would be an extremely busy two months. Captain FitzRoy would never dream of sailing into home base without the *Beagle* looking her very best. This meant that all hands were required on deck to scrub, polish, and paint, transforming the vessel back into what she had looked like five years ago, before she set out on her long adventure. Then and only then would the captain give the command to sail into English waters.

"England, our beloved England. Oh, to be in glorious England! Mr. Darwin!" the captain called to Charles, as they first sighted the green hills on the horizon. "Our voyage is finally coming to an end."

Charles looked around at the weary crew, who had suddenly come to life at the sight of their homeland. They had sailed around the world, and now, almost five years later, they were finally going home. *Who wouldn't have been excited?* thought Charles.

It was on October 2, 1836, that the *Beagle* anchored off Falmouth in Cornwall. A very tearful, sad farewell was exchanged between all as each crew member headed his separate way. Their adventure together had finally come to an end. Most joined other ships and sailed off to exotic parts of the world again.

Charles decided to settle down in London to try to regain some of the strength he had lost during his illness at sea. He needed to think about what he was going to do with the incredible amount of material he had collected on his travels. He thought that maybe he would write several articles and have them published in some of the scientific journals or, better still, write an entire book on what he had observed abroad, in those far-off, distant places.

He even thought of writing a few articles and submitting them to the medical journals to which his father subscribed.

Chapter Nine
The Origin of Species

Charles found it very difficult to relax after his voyage, so he spent most of his time studying specimens, doing experiments, then writing about his findings. He was a painstaking perfectionist, collecting and classifying his information endlessly. Although he was busy with his current work, he continued to puzzle over the problem of the finches and other questions related to them.

In 1844 Charles began formulating his material and setting out his ideas in book form. He would publish a book to let the world know that he had proof that plants and animals have slowly changed and developed, or evolved, over thousands of years. He was well aware that most people thought the Earth (and all forms of life on it) was created about six thousand years ago and that each species of animal and plant was created exactly as it is today. He also knew that what he intended to publish would cause violent debate among the scientific world as well as the general public. He would be attacking the general belief of so many people.

Charles became so involved in collecting examples and writing about them, to strengthen his case of evolution, that it took him fifteen years before he was somewhat satisfied that he had enough proof to warrant publishing a book on the subject. In 1859, *The Origin of Species* was published. It amazed Charles that the whole first edition of 1,250 copies sold on the first day of issue.

Charles tried to convey to his readers what he had discovered on the Galapagos Islands. He stated that in each kind of species there were offspring slightly different from their parents and these, in turn, produced offspring slightly different from themselves. He explained that the reason why the world was not now crowded with strange-looking creatures is because those offspring with variations suited to their environment survived. Others died off. In this way animals and plants evolved to what they are today.

This new theory about life caused much anger both in England and around the rest of the world. Charles was violently accused of being a radical naturalist by many people. They demanded that he keep his outrageous thoughts to himself.

Charles, in fact, was not too disturbed by the criticism and continued his quiet study of nature at his home in Downe, Kent. He paid little attention to what people were saying about him. In fact, he was so excited about his book that he decided to write another one, *The Descent of Man*, published twelve years later, in 1871. This aroused fresh and still more unfriendly criticism for Charles, because in it he said that man has the same ancestors as chimpanzees and apes.

He ignored what the Bible says about the creation of man, because he wanted a scientific way to explain the evolution of man.

There wasn't a science journal or newspaper around the word that didn't carry a story about Charles. People were furious with him because they believed that man was not related to any other animal, let alone an ape. Charles did not mind; he wasn't too affected by the controversy. For one thing, he was very gentle and the kindliest of men, who would go to any length to avoid confrontation with someone over this theories.

In 1839, Charles married his cousin Emma Wedgwood. They lived in London until 1842, when bad health caused Charles to move to Downe. There he lived and worked for the rest of his life. They had ten children, three of whom died in infancy.

It wasn't too long before the world of science was won over by Charles's notion of evolution by natural selection. Today the general idea of evolution is accepted by science everywhere.

Charles died in Downe, Kent, England, on April 19, 1882. He was buried in Westminster Abbey on April 26, 1882.

At the height of Charles's popularity he was often heard saying, "If only my father could see me now."